Alfred's Teach Yourself Guitar Repair & Maintenance

JOHN CARRUTHERS

Everything you need to know to start working on your guitar!

Alfred, the leader in educational publishing, and the National Guitar Workshop, one of America's finest guitar schools, have joined forces to bring you the best, most progressive educational tools possible. We hope you will enjoy this book and encourage you to look for other fine products from Alfred and the National Guitar Workshop.

This book was acquired, edited and produced by Workshop Arts, Inc., the publishing arm of the National Guitar Workshop.
Nathaniel Gunod, managing and acquisitions editor
Timothy Phelps, interior design

Cover photographs by Karen Miller.
Interior photographs by Larry Lytle.

ISBN 0-7390-3603-3 (Book & DVD)
ISBN 0-7390-3601-7 (Book)

CONTENTS

ABOUT THE AUTHOR

John Carruthers started repairing and building guitars nearly 40 years ago in a converted garage in West Los Angeles. Over the years, John has built a reputation among players and manufacturers for his knowledge and quality workmanship. John was a staff writer for Guitar Player magazine for nearly ten years, authoring the guitar workshop column and writing product reviews.

John's many inventions include products and techniques like the multi-saddle compensated bridge for acoustic guitars and basses used by such companies as Takamine, Lowden and Guild. Another of his innovations is a stereo pickup system for acoustic guitars using a microphone and piezo transducer or magnetic soundhole pickup. He designed and built the neck-duplicating machine currently used by the Fender custom shop.

John has done consulting and prototype work for many manufacturers including Fender, Music Man, Yamaha, Ibanez, G&L and EMG. Some of his more notable projects include working with artists on their signature models. John has worked with such noted players as Joe Pass, Lee Ritenour, Robben Ford, Eric Clapton, Eddie Van Halen, Steve Vai and many more. Carruthers Guitars currently occupies a modern, 5000 square foot repair and manufacturing facility in Venice, California and continues to repair and build high-quality instruments under John's leadership.

INTRODUCTION

Most guitarists are unfamiliar adjusting or maintaining their guitar. This is unfortunate because proper adjustment and maintenance of their instrument will enhance the sound and playability while prolonging its life. Even the simplest task, such as changing the strings properly, can pose great difficulty to someone who has not been shown the proper method. In this book, we will show you the best ways to string, polish and adjust your instrument.

PARTS OF THE GUITAR

Headstock

Tuning machines

Capstan

String retainer

Nut

Frets

Pickups

Saddles

Bridge

Pickup selector

Tremolo arr

Controls, tone and volume

Tailpiece

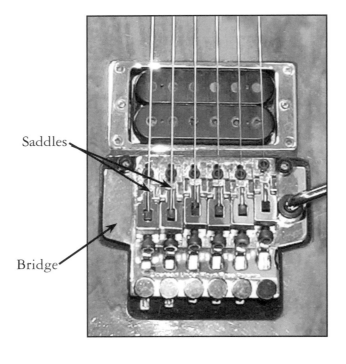

Saddles

Bridge

GENERAL SETUP

CHANGING THE STRINGS

Before attempting to setup your guitar, it is very important to install new strings. As strings get old they become corroded, filled with oils and perspiration and dented by the frets. This will cause the string to vibrate in an erratic manner and interfere with proper intonation and action adjustment.

Removing Old Strings

First, remove the old strings from your guitar. The best way to do this will vary with the type of bridge assembly you have.

For guitars with locking tremolos, you should start with Step 1. With other guitars, proceed to Step 3.

Step 1: Release the locking nut.

Step 2: Insert a spacer (see photo) between the rear edge of the bridge and the top of the guitar. This will stabilize the floating motion and make re-tuning much easier. You can use a piece of wooden doweling or cork.

Step 3: De-tune the strings until slack. Release the string locks on the bridge saddles and remove the strings. Be careful not to misplace any loose parts, floating bridges, nuts or other hardware.

After the strings have been removed is a perfect opportunity to clean and polish your guitar (see pages 39–45).

Installing New Strings

The proper installation of strings is very important! It will help eliminate the number one source of tuning problems and string breakage: poorly installed strings.

Most electric guitars with conventional tuning machines can be strung the same way:

Step 1: Insert the string through the appropriate hole in the tailpiece, guide it over the saddle and nut, then insert it through the hole in the capstan.

Step 2: With your left hand maintaining tension on the string past the tuning gear, and your right hand grasping the string midway down the neck, create enough slack above the fingerboard (approx. 3" or 76.2 mm*) to allow sufficient winds on the capstan. As you lift the string at the midpoint of the fingerboard, use your index finger to gauge the proper distance. This should allow approximately two-to-three turns around the capstan.

This will ensure a strong hold on the string while reducing the chance of breakage due to a concentration of stress.

Using your index finger to gauge proper amount of slack.

* Millimeters

Step 3: "Lock" the string by bringing the loose end over the capstan towards the center of the headstock and looping it under the captured string between the nut and the capstan.

Step 4: Next, bend the string up and back toward the middle of the neck.

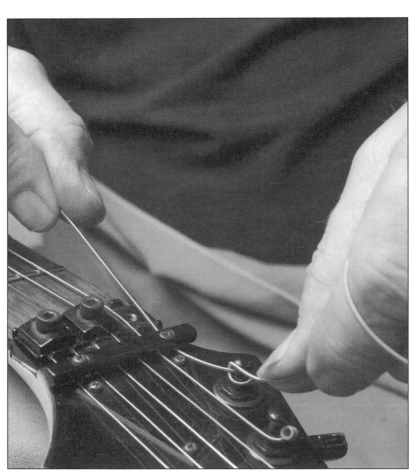

Step 5: While maintaining tension on the string with your right hand, wind the string in a downward spiral onto the capstan. Once the string comes to tension, you may release your right hand.

Step 6: Using wire cutters, cut off the excess string.

Locking Tuners

There are two types of locking tuners: manual and auto. Manual tuners require the player to insert the string in the capstan hole, take up the slack and then manually lock the knob on the back of the tuner. Auto lockers require no action on the part of the player—just insert the string through the capstan, take up the slack and tune to pitch. (Guitars equipped with locking tremolo systems require a different procedure—see page 62.)

Manual Locking Tuner

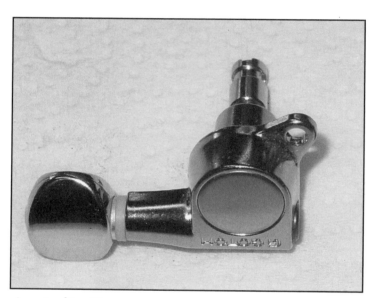

Auto Locking Tuner

Stretching the Strings

Stretching the strings will help them stay in tune. If you have a Floyd Rose system, before locking the nut, it is advisable to adjust your fine tuners to nearly the full out position before stretching your strings.

Step 1: Grasp the string between the thumb and the first finger of the picking hand.

Step 2: Raise the string *slightly* above the fingerboard, sliding your fingers and thumb along the length of the string while maintaining this outward position. Don't over-stretch the string, as it might break.

Step 3: Retune and repeat this procedure until the tuning stabilizes.

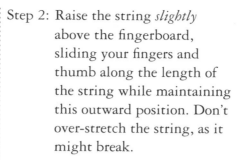

Step 4: Finally, if you have a Floyd Rose, lock the nut clamps with an Allen wrench.

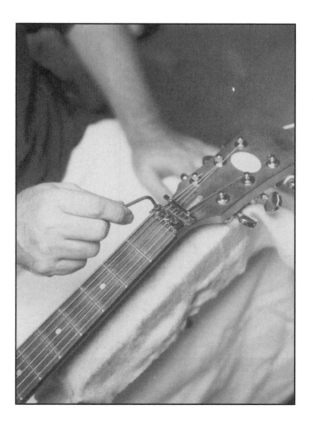

Stringing Fender Slotted Machine Heads

Some Fender guitars and basses have tuning machines with a slotted capstan. This style of machine head requires a different method of stringing.

It is necessary to allow slightly more slack than with normal tuning machines (approximately 5" or 12.5 cm).

Step 1: Bend the end of the string 90 degrees and cut to length.

Step 2: Insert the bent end into the capstan as shown in the photograph on the right.

Step 3: While maintaining tension on the string with your right hand, wind the string in a downward spiral onto the capstan.

On basses, the procedure is the same except you must leave more slack due to the increased diameter of the capstan and strings. The bass strings should extend approximately 8" or about 18 cm. past the capstan.

NOTE

In both cases it is advisable to bend the string before cutting. This prevents the outer wraps from slipping and the string from going dead.

TRUSS ROD ADJUSTMENT

The first step in setting up a guitar should be the truss rod adjustment. Before getting started, the guitar should be strung with the brand and gauge of strings you prefer and tuned to pitch. Depending on how your guitar is made, you will need an Allen wrench, a screwdriver or a socket driver.

The truss rod adjustment changes the bow (curve) of the neck and affects all other adjustments, including action and intonation. A nut for adjusting the truss rod appears at the head or at the heel of the guitar.

Contrary to popular belief, guitar necks must have a certain amount of inward bow to play properly. Strings vibrate in slow curves with the largest curve being at their midpoint. Having a small amount of bow in the neck accommodates this motion. Too much bow has a sharping affect on the strings, since it increases the distance a string must stretch to reach the fret. It makes playing more difficult for the same reason. A reverse bow (outward) causes the strings to buzz against the frets in the lower registers (closer to the nut).

Bow

Reverse or Back Bow

NOTE

All guitar necks must have a little bow. In this illustration, the bow is exaggerated for the purpose of demonstration.

Direction of Adjustment

With most truss rods, bow is reduced by turning the adjustment-nut clockwise, strengthening the neck. Counterclockwise movement causes a relaxation in the neck, increasing the natural bow created by string tension. You should always face the screw and turn it in a clockwise or counterclockwise direction (depending on the desired adjustment) regardless of whether the adjustment-nut appears at the head or at the heel of the guitar.

Remember, you must have full string tension on the neck when measuring the amount of curvature and making these adjustments. The tension of the strings is the primary factor creating the bow.

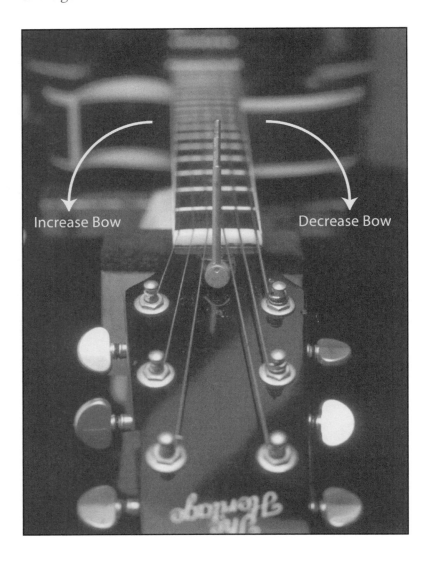

Testing for the Proper Amount of Bow

To test the amount of bow, press down a string simultaneously at the 1st fret and at the fret where the neck joins the body. The amount of bow is the space between that string and the top of the fret lying halfway between the points you are pressing.

For example, if your neck joins the body at the 19th fret, put your guitar on a flat surface and touch the 1st and 19th frets simultaneously—the distance between the string and the top of the 9th fret is the amount of bow. You will need a set of feeler gauges to measure this gap.

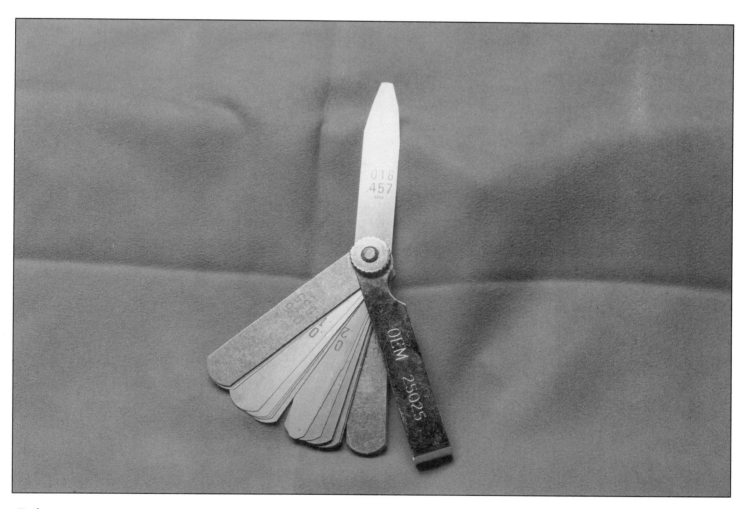

Feeler gauges.

You will need a free hand. You can use a capo to hold the string down at the 1st fret while your other hand touches the string at the point where the neck joins the body, leaving one hand free to measure the bow.

Set the capo just tight enough to touch the strings to the fret. Too much pressure can cause an arch in the string, resulting in a false reading.

To get accurate measurements:

1. String the guitar with the brand and gauge of strings you use.

2. All strings must be on the guitar.

3. The instrument must be tuned to pitch.

Close-up of feeler gauge measuring the distance between fret and string.

Measuring the Amount of Bow

The procedure for measuring the amount of bow is the same for electric, bass and acoustic guitars, though height specifications will vary. The amount of bow necessary depends on the type and particular characteristics of the instrument, balanced against the needs and demands of the player. However, the following guidelines provide a basic adjustment that will usually suffice:

Having pressed the two points on the string as indicated on page 16, find the midway spot and measure between the string and the top of the fret (the sixth string is usually the most convenient for this). Most repairmen use a mechanic's feeler gauge—the kind used for adjusting points and valves on cars. The following basic standards tend to be the most useful for the widest variety of guitars and playing styles:

For acoustic and electric guitars: .010" (.254 mm).

For bass guitars: .015" (.381 mm). See note below.

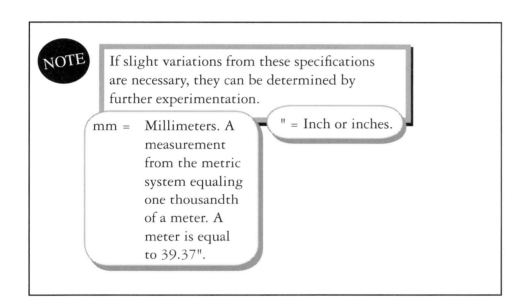

NOTE If slight variations from these specifications are necessary, they can be determined by further experimentation.

mm = Millimeters. A measurement from the metric system equaling one thousandth of a meter. A meter is equal to 39.37".

" = Inch or inches.

In fact, this is one area where you may wish merely to understand the process and leave the actual adjustment to a skilled repairman. The amount of adjustment on the truss rod is very critical, and too much movement can either break the rod or cause a back bow. Usually it takes very little adjustment to achieve the correct amount of bow. These adjustments change the stresses on the instrument. It is advisable to recheck your measurements after a short period of time, to be sure that the neck has properly settled.

CAUTION

All adjustments should be carried out in small increments and very carefully.

ADJUSTING THE ACTION AT THE BRIDGE

Before you begin to adjust the action at the bridge, the guitar should be strung with the brand and gauge of strings you prefer and tuned to pitch. The degree of tension and specific playing properties of the strings affect action height by stressing the neck.

Necessary Tools

The only tools ordinarily required for these adjustments on electric guitars and basses are:

- Small screwdrivers and/or Allen wrenches of appropriate sizes for the bridge adjustment screws

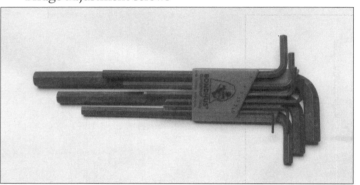

- Studs or set screws (either Allen or slotted type)

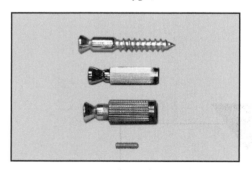

- A scale (ruler)

These tools are all available at your music dealer or at hardware stores. Allen wrenches are frequently supplied with the guitar.

Measuring Action Height at the Upper End of the Fingerboard

It is best to make this measurement while holding the guitar in playing position. When resting on a bench, the weight of the guitar may affect the neck position making the reading inaccurate.

Place the end of a steel rule (a 6" stainless steel ruler with $1/64"$ as its smallest increment) on top of the 12th fret. Look across the fingerboard to measure the gap between the top of the indicated fret and the bottom of the string you are checking.

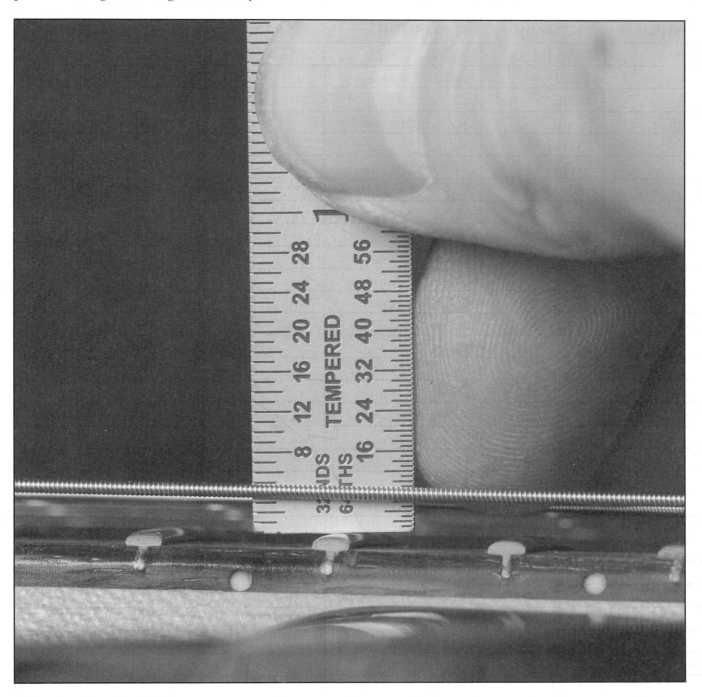

Measuring the action height.

Setup Specifications

Use this chart to help determine the proper action height for each string of your instrument.

Some players require action that may vary from the chart due to individual playing styles in combination with the variable characteristics of their instrument. The specifications in the chart work well with most instruments and playing styles, and provide a reference to make changes from.

Guitar	String	Action*	Nut Action	Truss Rod
Electrics	1st (high)	4/64" or 1.587 mm	.018" or .457 mm	.010" or .254 mm
	2nd	4/64" or 1.587 mm		
	3rd	4/64" or 1.587 mm		
	4th	4/64" or 1.587 mm		
	5th	5/64" or 1.984 mm		
	6th (low)	5/64" or 1.984 mm		
Acoustics	1st (high)	4/64" or 1.587 mm	.022" or .558 mm	.010" or .254 mm
	2nd	4/64" or 1.587 mm		
	3rd	5/64" or 1.984 mm		
	4th	5/64" or 1.984 mm		
	5th	6/64" or 2.381 mm		
	6th (low)	6/64" or 2.381 mm		
4-String Bass	1st (high)	6/64" or 2.381 mm	.022" or .558 mm	.015" or .381 mm
	2nd	7/64" or 2.778 mm		
	3rd	8/64" or 3.175 mm		
	4th (low)	8/64" or 3.175 mm		
5-String Bass	1st (high)	6/64" or 2.381 mm	.022" or .558 mm	.015" or .381 mm
	2nd	7/64" or 2.778 mm		
	3rd	8/64" or 3.175 mm		
	4th	9/64" or 3.572 mm		
	5th (low)	10/64" or 3.969 mm		
6-String Bass	1st (high)	6/64" or 2.381 mm	.022" or .558 mm	.015" or .381 mm
	2nd	7/64" or 2.778 mm		
	3rd	8/64" or 3.175 mm		
	4th	9/64" or 3.572 mm		
	5th	9/64" or 3.572 mm		
	6th (low)	10/64" or 3.969 mm		
Fretless Bass	1st (high)	6/64" or 2.381 mm	.020" or .508 mm	.010" or .254 mm
	2nd	7/64" or 2.778 mm		
	3rd	8/64" or 3.175 mm		
	4th (low)	8/64" or 3.175 mm		

* Measured at the 12th fret.

Making the Adjustments

Electric guitar bridges are of two basic designs. The simplest type has adjustment wheels or studs on each end of a single saddle. It relies on a preset *curvature*.

Curvature refers to the height of the bridge saddles, which are not equal all the way across. Usually, saddles are slightly higher in the middle. This curvature should correspond to the curvature of the fingerboard. By adjusting each end of the bridge to the required specifications, the strings in the middle automatically arrive at the proper specifications.

Adjustments for fixed curvature bridges are done in the following manner:

Step 1: Determine the measurements for the 1st and 6th strings from the setup chart on page 20.

Step 2: Measure the action on your guitar as described on page 19.

Step 3: Adjust the studs or thumb wheels until your guitar matches the specifications.

Clockwise rotation of the stud or thumb wheel lowers the action, and counterclockwise movement raises it.

CAUTION

Some stud-type bridges have locking screws that should be released before making height adjustments. Your owner's manual will tell you how to do this.

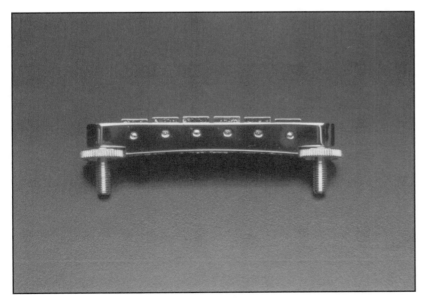

A thumb-wheel bridge.

The other type of bridge has individually adjustable saddles. Each saddle must be adjusted for the proper clearance from the fret.

Adjustments for bridges with individual saddles are done in the following manner:

Step 1: Determine the measurements for the 1st through 6th strings from the setup chart on page 20.

Step 2: Measure the action on your guitar as described on page 19.

Step 3: Adjust both screws so the saddle remains parallel to the base plate. This will maintain proper string spacing.

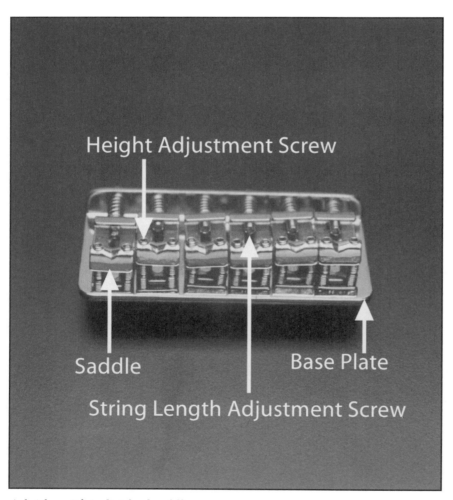

A *bridge with individual saddles.*

Usually, with this type of bridge, clockwise rotation raises the string and counterclockwise rotation lowers the string.

Adjustments for electric basses are done the same way but with different specifications (see page 20).

ADJUSTING THE ACTION AT THE NUT

After setting the action at the bridge, the next step is to set the action at the nut. Remember, the guitar should be strung with the brand and gauge of strings you prefer and tuned to pitch.

Bone, Plastic or Graphite Nuts

Necessary Tools

To measure action height at the nut, you should use the same "feeler gauge" set that you used for measuring the truss rod adjustment. You will require gauge blades between .018" (.457 mm) to .022" (.559 mm).

Adjusting the action at the nut involves actually cutting the nut slots deeper. For this, you can use X-acto saws for the treble strings and nut files for the bass strings. X-acto saws are available from hobby shops, hardware stores or luthier's suppliers. The nut file is a specialized guitar repairman's tool. They are available from luthier's suppliers or industrial suppliers. Both X-acto saws and nut files come in varying widths to accommodate different string gauges. It is necessary to select a blade or file that is slightly wider than the string to prevent the string from binding in the nut.

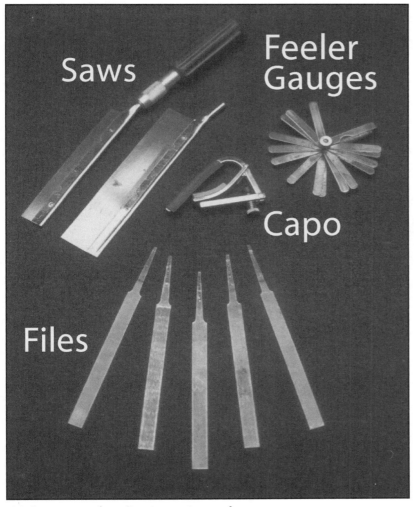

Tools necessary for adjusting action at the nut.

Measuring Action
at the 1st Fret

Measurements to determine proper action at the nut are done with a feeler gauge at the 1st fret. Hold the gauge parallel to the string surface to get an accurate measurement.

Step 1: Select the proper feeler gauge blade from the specification chart on page 20.

Step 2: Insert the blade between the string and the first fret. You must hold the gauge parallel to the string surface to insure an accurate measurement.

Measuring the nut action.

For electric guitars, .018" (.4572 mm) between the first fret and the bottom of each string is usually an ideal height—low enough to be comfortable, but high enough to avoid buzzing. For basses and acoustic guitars, use .022" (.5588 mm).

Lower or higher settings than these may be used, depending on the instrument's resonance factor, structural strength, type of strings used, etc., but these recommended heights will work well for most players.

Re-Slotting to Specifications

Step 1: Check the nut height (measured at the 1st fret).

Step 2: If the string is too high, you must carefully re-slot the nut deeper by cutting with an X-acto saw or file.

Step 3: Re-measure and cut until the gauge touches both fret and string, yet does not push the string upward. The fit should be exact.

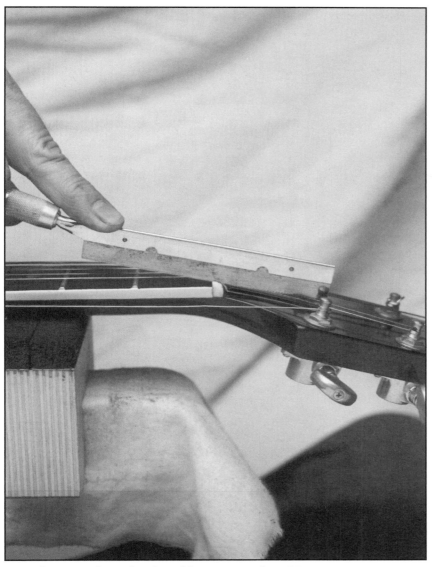

Cut the groove deeper for the treble strings with an X-acto saw.

Cut the groove deeper for the bass strings with a nut file.

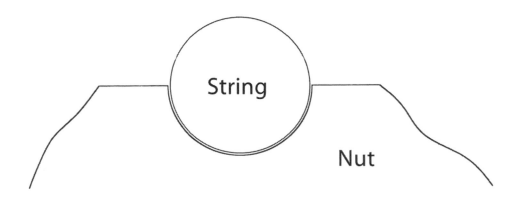

The fit should be exact.

Important Rules

Rule 1: Remember, it takes very little cutting to lower the string! Unfortunately, it's easier to remove material (by cutting too deep) than it is to replace it.

Rule 2: The angle of the nut slot is very important. The nut slots should be cut at the same angle as that of the string from the nut to the capstan. This will insure proper downward pressure and that the string departs properly from the edge of the nut facing the fingerboard. (See photo below).

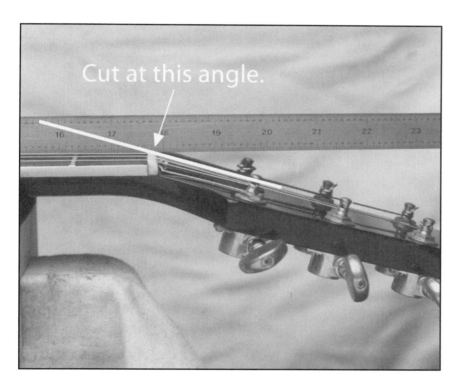

Cut at this angle.

The nut slots should be cut at the same angle as the string creates from the nut to the capstan.

Rule 3: Proceed cautiously, cutting small amounts and then re-measuring. Repeat the process until the adjustment is correct. Remember to restore full tension to the string each time you re-measure.

Rule 4: **Remember!** Make sure that the string is fully seated in the slot each time you take a measurement. If your saw or file sizing isn't correct, the string may wedge above the bottom of the slot resulting in a flawed measurement. If you don't notice this and keep cutting, you will make the slot too deep and ruin the nut.

If the Slot is Too Deep — Shimming the Nut

Buzzes caused by the nut slot being too low occur only when the string is played open. To determine whether you have a nut buzz or a saddle buzz, press a string at the first fret so that the string vibrates between that fret and the bridge. If the buzz is gone, you have a nut buzz. The nut may have to be shimmed or replaced.

Putting glue in the slots to shim up the string is not recommended. This makeshift approach is temporary and unreliable. It is more advisable to raise the entire nut by placing shims under it and regluing it in position, then reslotting until the proper height is achieved for all strings. Shims are typically made of plastic, sheet metal or even heavy paper, such as pieces of file folder material.

▼ CAUTION

An expert should remove a bone, plastic or graphite nut for shimming. Attempts by the inexperienced often cause irreparable damage to the nut channel or to the finish surrounding it.

Mechanical Nuts

Electric guitars with mechanical nuts require different adjustment procedures. Adjustments are made by adding or removing shims under the nut assembly.

The Measurements for Mechanical Nuts

Step 1: Measure and record the height of each string from the 1st fret.

Step 2: Note if the strings are all the same height from the 1st fret. This will help to determine if the nut follows the curvature of the fingerboard. If the middle strings are closer to the first fret than the outside two the nut doesn't conform to the curvature.

Interpreting the Measurements

1. If the nut is too high, subtract the standard specification from the measured overage. This will be the amount of shim you will have to remove.

2. Conversely, if the nut height is too low, some shims will have to be added until the proper specification is reached.

3. In the case where the curvature of the nut doesn't conform to the curvature of the neck, the action must be adjusted using the height specification of the lowest string.

4. If the strings conform to the fingerboard, the action can be adjusted by adding or removing shims to each end until the proper height is achieved.

5. If the nut is too high with no shims, it will be necessary to remove wood from the nut slot. **To avoid cosmetic damage to the instrument, an expert should do this.**

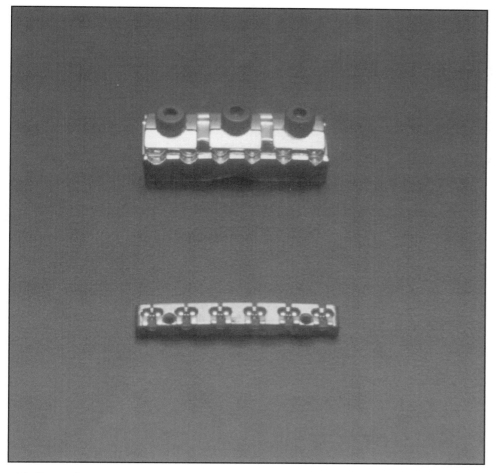

Mechanical nuts.

Making the Adjustments

For a guitar without a locking trem, go directly to Step 2.

Step 1: On a guitar with a locking trem, loosen and remove nut locks.

Step 2: Loosen the strings until slack. (If you have a floating trem, don't forget the spacer at the bridge!)

Step 3: Loosen and remove the screws on the back of the neck that hold the nut assembly.

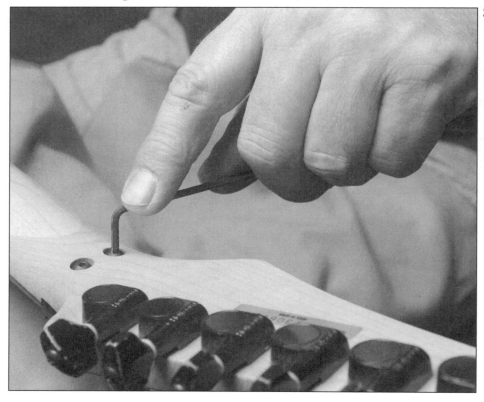

Step 4: Carefully remove the nut assembly, noting the position and height of existing shims.

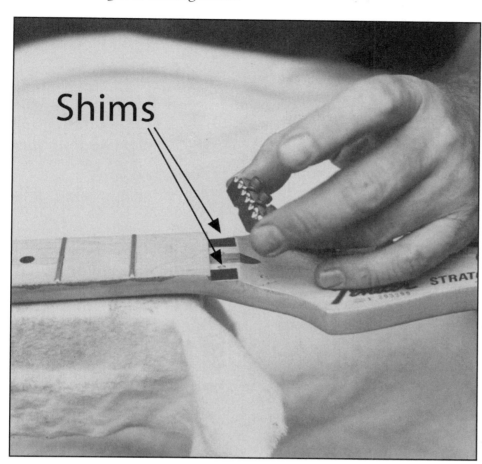

Placing shims under the nut.

Step 5: Add or subtract the appropriate shims to arrive at the proper specification.

Step 6: Reattach the nut assembly and tune the strings to pitch. Stretch and retune. Lock the nut clamps.

Industrial supply stores sell shim stock. It is made of thin sheets of metal that can be cut with scissors. It comes in varying thicknesses, calibrated to a thousandth of an inch.

INTONATION

It is not unusual for guitarists to find that, despite their best efforts, their guitar will not play in tune. It may be in tune in the open position but in higher positions one or all of the strings are out of tune. This frustrating situation is usually related to the vibrating string length, which is measured from the nut to the bridge. This section is about how to check your intonation and change the string length to correct it.

Basic Principles of String Length

1. Too short a string length will cause a string to be sharp (sound slightly higher in pitch) as you move up into higher positions.

2. Too long a string length will cause a string to go flat (sound slightly lower in pitch) as you move up into higher positions.

The vibrating string length is measured from nut to bridge.

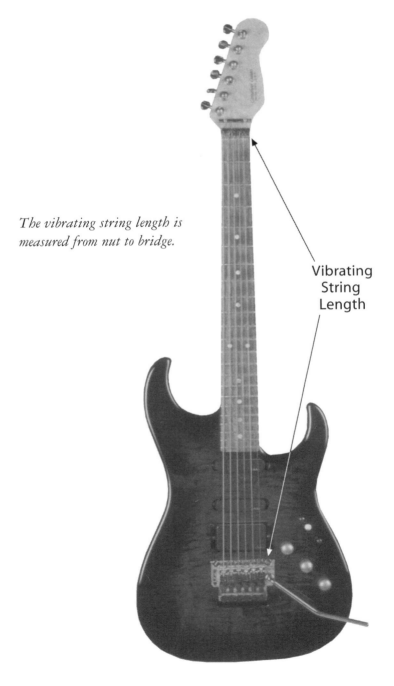

Vibrating String Length

Electronic Tuners

There are several types of electronic tuning devices that can be used for checking intonation. They translate the incoming signal (i.e., musical note) into a visual image that accurately indicates whether the note is being played on pitch, sharp, or flat.

Basic Rules of Operation:

1. When the note being played is on pitch, the indicator holds on center.

2. Movement to the left indicates flatness.

3. Movement to the right indicates sharpness.

Tuners work in various ways. The most commonly used tuners use a *sample and hold* technology, meaning the signal is sampled several times, analyzed and then displayed. Sample and hold-type tuners include:

Meter: which has a needle that stands up straight if the signal is in tune.

Light pulsation or stroboscopic: which has a row of lights that lock in the center when the signal is in tune.

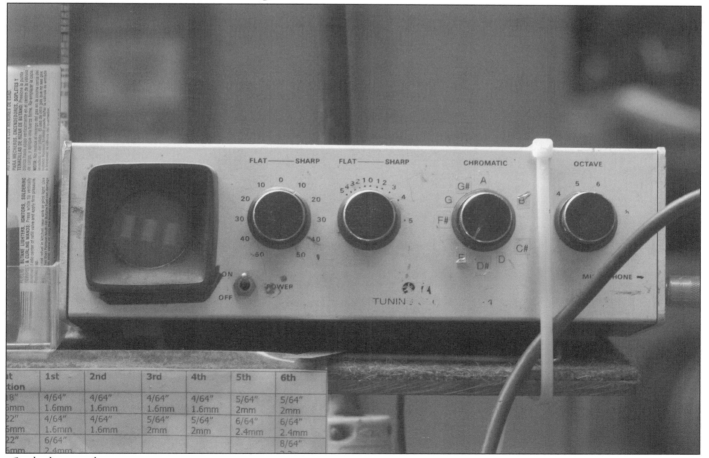

t tion	1st	2nd	3rd	4th	5th	6th
8" 5mm	4/64" 1.6mm	4/64" 1.6mm	4/64" 1.6mm	4/64" 1.6mm	5/64" 2mm	5/64" 2mm
22" 5mm	4/64" 1.6mm	4/64" 1.6mm	5/64" 2mm	5/64" 2mm	6/64" 2.4mm	6/64" 2.4mm
22" 5mm	6/64" 2.4mm					8/64"

Cathode ray tube tuner.

Since these tuners are sampling several times before displaying results, they do not work in real time—the results are delayed. Other less commonly used tuners work in real time. They include:

Cathode Ray Tube: which has a square pattern that locks in the middle of a screen when the signal is in tune.

Stroboscopic: which displays a rotating disc on a screen that appears to stop when in tune.

On stroboscopic tuners, the speed of movement to the right or left indicates the relative degree of sharpness or flatness. If the indicator moves very quickly to the left, the intonation is more flat. If the indicator moves very slowly to the left, the intonation is less flat. Due to the device's extreme sensitivity to the slightest irregularities in the string, there may be small movements around the center point of the indicator even when the string is in tune. When the string is in tune, the movement is equidistant from the center.

Reasons to Use an Electronic Tuner:

Electronic tuning devices are far more accurate than the human ear because they:

1. Detect much smaller frequency changes.

2. Register only the actual pitch of the note, while the ear often has difficulty because tone quality and overtones obscure pitch.

3. Are a consistent reference for *absolute pitch*.

Absolute pitch refers to the exact frequency of a note. In other words, "A" is "A" because it is 440 Hz (hertz, or cycles per second). Relative pitch has to do with how one note compares to another.

The stroboscopic devices are usually accurate to within one *cent* ($^1/_{100}$ of a *half step*). A half step is the distance of one fret. Even some of the simpler and less expensive devices are accurate to within five cents.

If you frequently do your own intonation adjustments, a quality tuning device can be a worthwhile investment. They are also very useful for general tuning, especially on stage where ambient sound can make it difficult to hear whether or not you are in tune.

Typical sample and hold-type electronic tuning devices.

Finger Pressure and Intonation

Be careful not to press too hard. Applying too much pressure to a string can stretch it downward into the fingerboard. This makes the pitch go sharp. Misplacement of the fingers on the strings can also cause you to pull the string slightly off center, as in bending a string, with the same undesirable result. Proper finger pressure is just enough so that the string touches the fret firmly. Remember to place your fingers in close proximity to the fret. This will give you the leverage you need to secure the string against the fret without pressing too hard. To learn proper finger pressure, try this experiment:

Step 1: In normal playing position, place a finger on the 6th (lowest) string, in close proximity to the 5th fret, *but do not press. Just lightly touch the string.*

Step 2: Begin to apply pressure very slowly, in small increments, plucking all the while. At first, you will produce unpitched percussive sounds. Then, you will produce a slightly buzzy, unclear tone.

Step 3: The next tiny increment of pressure you apply should get you a clear, ringing sound.

NOTE

This is as hard as you need to press any note!

Pressing harder will cause your notes to sound sharp!

Excess finger pressure may cause the string to be displaced and sound sharp.

Testing and Adjusting Intonation

Tips for Using Tuning Devices to Test Intonation

Step 1: Before using the tuning device, be sure it is properly calibrated (follow the manufacturer's directions).

Step 2: Install new strings (see page 76). As strings get old they become corroded, filled or covered with body oils and dented by the frets. All of these factors inhibit normal vibration of the string and cause false readings.

Step 3: Lower the pickups away from the strings to avoid excess magnetic pull. Magnetic pull can cause erratic string vibration, making it impossible to achieve proper intonation.

Step 4: Pre-tune the guitar to concert pitch (A=440). This step is important for two reasons. First, it is necessary to have full tension on the neck when making adjustments since tension affects action and therefore intonation. Second, a string that is not tuned to correct pitch may produce a false reading on the tuner. Some tuning devices pick up and register harmonic overtones. For example, if the tuner is set to "E," a string tuned accidentally to "A" could produce a stable pattern on the indicator because "A" is a natural overtone of "E." By pre-tuning the guitar, you ensure that the indicator is registering the proper note.

With tuners that have auto-seek, one need only be concerned with tuning to the proper octave.

Step 5: Hold the guitar in normal playing position when testing intonation. Holding the guitar adds slight stresses to the neck and body and these stresses affect intonation. Testing in this way ensures adjustments that compensate for playing conditions.

Step 6: For electric guitars and basses, use a standard patch cord to plug directly into the tuning device. Set the pickup selector switch to the neck position and volume and tone controls to the full position. This will ensure maximum signal. For acoustic guitars, you can use the tuner's internal microphone.

Step 7: Use the 12th fret harmonic instead of the open string when tuning with the device. The harmonic creates more vibrations per second, causing a more continuous signal and therefore a clearer signal.

Now that you know about tuners and finger pressure, and have followed the steps as described on page 36, you are ready to test and correct your intonation.

The Test—Part 1

Step 1: Play the harmonic at the 12th fret. Tune the string until the tuner registers proper pitch.

Step 2: Play the note at the 12th fret of the string you just tuned. *Do not press too hard!* Take note if the string registers sharp or flat on the tuner. Do this several times to get the best average.

The Adjustment

If the fretted note is flat, the string is too long and must be shortened. If the fretted note is sharp, the string is too short and must be lengthened. To change the string length, you must adjust the saddle intonation screw. Clockwise rotation lengthens the string, and counterclockwise shortens the string.

Setting the string length adjustment screw (intonation). Be careful not to damage the front of the guitar with the shaft of the screwdriver.

On some bridges, there may be a saddle lock screw that must be released before making adjustments.

On "Floyd Rose" style systems, the string must be de-tuned before loosening the saddle lock screw. Set the string length adjustment and re-lock prior to retuning.

On some other bridges without intonation adjustment screws, loosen the saddle lock screws, move the saddle to the correct position and lock in place.

The Test—Part 2

Step 3: Retune the string to the open 12th fret harmonic and repeat Steps 1 and 2. When the open 12th fret harmonic and the fretted octave are the same, the intonation is on.

Step 4: Repeat Steps 1 through 3 on the rest of the strings.

NOTE

Thin strings flex right at the saddle, while stiffer strings don't. Because of this physical property, stiff strings must be longer to play in tune.

Acoustic Guitars

Unfortunately, most acoustic guitars can't be adjusted this way. To change the string length, a repairman may have to alter or move the saddle to a different position. This kind of work can be further complicated on acoustic guitars with pickups under or built into the saddle. You can test your acoustic guitar intonation but you should let a professional fix it!

CLEANING AND POLISHING YOUR GUITAR

Caring for your guitar's finish is a relatively simple procedure, but one which must be carried out with the proper materials and an understanding of their use. Prior to restringing is an appropriate time to polish your guitar (see page 5–6). Periodic maintenance of the finish enhances the beauty of the instrument. It also helps to prevent permanent surface damage that may result from the cumulative effects of wear and grime.

The two areas of concern in finish maintenance are:

1. The finished surfaces of the neck and body.

2. The unfinished surface of the fingerboard.

This section will discuss cleaning of these surfaces and the application of appropriate waxes and polishes for protection and preservation.

CAUTION

Be sure to read and understand these procedures before applying any unknown or new substances to your guitar.

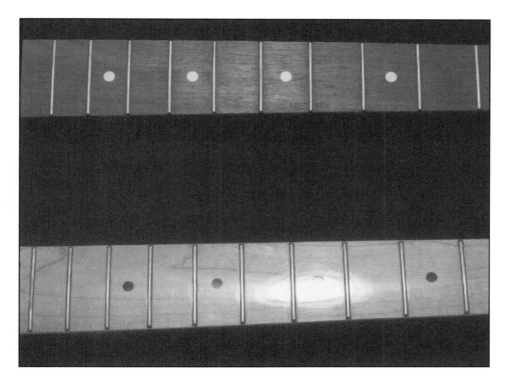

Some necks are unfinished (top) and others are finished (bottom).

Types of Finish

Guitars and other fretted instruments are finished with a variety of protective substances, the most common of which are nitrocellulose lacquer and synthetic finishes such as polyurethanes and polyesters. Most of these finishes are subject to oxidation and fading; all are subject to abrasion and the buildup of residues on the surface (grime, perspiration, wax, and smoke films).

If these effects are not dealt with regularly, they may lead to unnecessary and permanent damage to the guitar's finish.

Choosing the Correct Cleaning Solvent and Polish

Using a solvent or polish that is chemically incompatible with a given finish may cause irreparable damage. Some guitar and furniture polishes contain cleaning solvents as well as polishing and waxing agents; it is unsafe to assume that a polish will not react with the finish. Probably 95% of contemporary guitars are finished either in nitrocellulose lacquer or synthetics and lend themselves to the basic methods described here for cleaning and polishing. By testing first, you can avoid noticeable damage to the instrument from a reaction between the finish and the substance applied to it.

Testing Solvents, Cleaners and Polishes
Whatever the substance—water, chemical solvent, cleaning compound, wax or polish—test it on a small section of the guitar before working over the entire surface. For example, you can choose a small spot under a back plate or truss rod cover to test whether there will be a reaction between the substance and the finish. With the vast majority of guitars, it is highly unlikely that there will be any problem. In the rare case where there is a reaction, using this approach will assure that the damage will be slight. The chances of a reaction are extremely remote, but it is easier to be cautious in the first place than to correct substantial damage in the rare instance it does occur.

> **CAUTION**
>
> *Various manufacturers make "guitar polish" and such products are available at most music stores. Be very careful and do not assume that these are "safe." Test them carefully before committing to their use. It is a good idea to put a dab of the substance on a cloth instead of applying it directly to your guitar. Then, test it as described above.*

Polishing Cloths

All cleaning and polishing should be done with flannelette, a soft cotton material available at fabric stores. Do not use pre-treated flannelette cloths—they may harm the finish. Avoid using ordinary rag material or paper towels, as they may have an undesirable abrasive quality.

Step 1: Fold the cloth into a small pad for applying the solvent, cleaner or polish.

Step 2: Always do one section at a time, wiping it immediately with a clean, dry piece of cloth.

Use a flannette cloth to polish your guitar.

Flannelette can be washed and re-used, although washing lessens its softness.

Make sure that the cloths are free of debris, such as wood or metal particles, that might scratch the guitar's surface. Cloth used for one cleaning or polishing operation should not be used for another. For example, a cloth used with cleaning compounds will contain abrasives that will interfere with subsequent polishing and waxing.

Preliminary Cleaning with Damp and Dry Cloths

In most cases, some of the accumulated substances on the finished surface are water soluble, while others require a chemical solvent or cleaning compound.

As a matter of procedure, it is best to first carefully clean the surface with water before using chemical solvents or compounds.

One method is to slightly dampen a flannelette cloth and clean the finish one small section at a time, wiping immediately with a dry cloth after each application.

Clean one small section at a time.

Cleaning Lacquer and Synthetic Finishes with Chemical Solvents

After completing the steps explained on page 41, repeat the procedure using mineral spirits to dampen the flannelette cloth. Work on a small section at a time and clean it with a fresh dry cloth. Be sure to remove all residue before moving onto the next section. Mineral spirits are available at hardware and paint stores.

CAUTION

Always use solvents sparingly and carefully. Follow the safety instructions on the container.

Occasionally, the application of a chemical solvent will result in a thin hazy film on the surface of the guitar. This is usually due to oxidation or a wax residue that is resistant to the solvent. In such a case, the haze can be removed by application of cleaning compounds in accordance with the instructions on page 40.

Removing Oxides and Abrasions from Lacquered and Synthetic Finishes

In many cases, cleaning with water and chemical solvents will be sufficient to prepare the surface for final polishing or waxing. Sometimes oxidation of the finish has dulled it to such an extent that wax or polish alone will not restore it to a high luster, or there may be minor abrasions that mar its appearance.

After cleaning the entire finished surface of the instrument with water and solvent, you can determine the state of the finish. Oxidation or minor abrasions can be handled with a cleaning compound.

CAUTION

Deep marks, dents, abrasions or scratches cannot be removed in this manner. Such problems require expert attention— refinishing in most cases.

An excellent agent for removing minor abrasions or oxides and restoring depth and luster is any mild polishing compound that contains both mild abrasives and polishing agents. Reputable brands are available at auto supply and hardware stores.

Step 1: Place just a bit of compound on a flannelette cloth and work it over the finish, covering a small area at a time.

Step 2: Wipe immediately with a clean, dry flannelette cloth. Use small circular motions on solid colors; rub with the grain where it is visible. The amount of pressure should be light to moderate, depending on the severity of the problem to be corrected.

Step 3: Apply a second application of the compound, using lighter pressure. This will reduce the rubbing marks created by abrasives in the first application.

The compound will always leave small marks, but these should fill in when the polish or wax is applied. Nevertheless, use the compound sparingly and carefully, remembering that it removes a very thin layer of finish in order to expose fresh gloss.

Make sure all residues are removed before polishing and waxing. The use of a cleaning compound should be necessary no more than once every one or two years, depending on the guitar and its use. Exercise some restraint in deciding when to apply it. For example, if only one section of the guitar needs this treatment, refrain from using the compound on all the surfaces merely as a matter of routine, and apply it only when necessary.

Waxing and Polishing

Once the finish has been cleaned, gloss can be further restored and heightened with a high quality guitar or furniture polish. This will leave a strong shine that both enhances and protects the finish. Spray waxes and polishes are easy to use since you can spray a small amount onto the flannelette cloth and apply directly, but other liquid waxes and polishes are equally effective. Apply the polish sparingly, covering a small area at a time. Use different cloths for cleaning and polishing. Fingerboards with lacquer or synthetic finishes should be cleaned and polished with the same methods described above.

Work the steel wool across the fingerboard and frets, scrubbing perpendicular to the length of the neck. Be careful that the steel wool touches only the surface of the fingerboard and not the headstock, the finished portion of the neck or the body of the instrument. On electric guitars, put masking tape across the tops of the pickups so that the iron particles from the steel wool will not attach to the magnetic pole pieces (the particles may affect the functioning of the pickups).

Once the fingerboard is cleaned, the natural oils from the hands will lightly polish it in the course of playing. In most cases, this is all that is needed. However, if extra smoothness is desired, carnauba paste wax can be used on the fingerboard. Apply it in accordance with the directions provided with the product.

Cleaning and Polishing the Unfinished Fingerboard

Most unfinished fingerboards are made of rosewood or ebony. They should not be cleaned and polished in the same way finished fingerboards are, since raw wood requires special treatment. Certain substances contained in polishes and cleaners need to be avoided.

To clean the fingerboard, and to shine the frets simultaneously, use 0000 grade steel wool. This is the finest grade available.

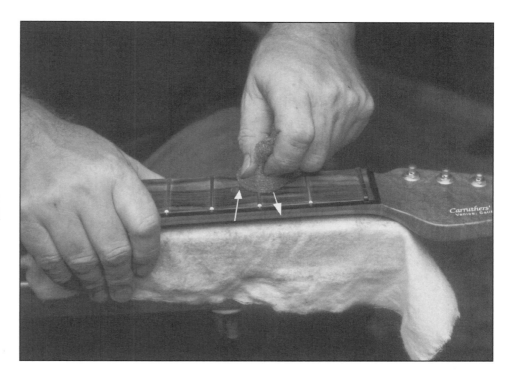

> **CAUTION**
>
> *Do **not** use a coarser grade than 0000 steel wool.*

> **CAUTION**
>
> *Never leave steel wool near a 9-volt battery as it can easily ignite.*

Routine Cleaning

You can reduce the need for revitalizing the finish by keeping the guitar in its case, wiping it down with a clean flannelette cloth after playing and avoiding exposure of the instrument to the elements. These practices should be followed with all types of guitars.

ELECTRONIC MAINTENANCE

Electric guitars and basses are subject to electronic problems. The most common problems are loose components, such as the jack or potentiometers, and corrosion.

In the case of loose components, the wires often break off due to fatigue caused by loose components moving around, such as potentiometers or jacks. To restore normal function, the wires must be reconnected. This is usually done by *soldering*.

In the case of corrosion, the components must be cleaned and lubricated or replaced.

Soldering

Soldering is a distinct form of low-temperature welding that provides a bond between two metal surfaces. Unlike some types of welding that fuse metals together, solder only fills in the spaces in and between adjacent metals. Solder is used to make a reliable electrical connection that will remain free from corrosion and have good conductance.

Most people know what soldering is, but very few know how to do it properly.

Basic Requirements for Soldering
1. The correct materials.

2. Proper tools.

3. Good preparation.

4. Correct technique.

Qualities of Solders
Solders are mixtures of low melting-point metals such as tin and lead. Varying the ratio of the different metals controls the melting point of the solder. Usually the solder has a core that is made from rosin. This cleans the metals to be joined and promotes the proper flow.

Solders come in different diameters. Normally the diameter is selected according to the size of the job. For example, if you were soldering on an intricate circuit board, you would want to use small diameter solder.

NOTE

Some solders have acid cores. This is undesirable for electrical connections.

Necessary Tools for
Soldering

1. A high quality soldering iron of the appropriate wattage.

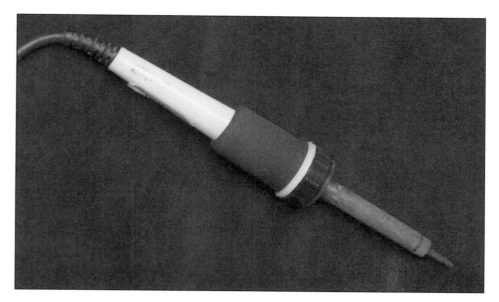

2. A cellulose sponge (for cleaning the tip of the soldering iron).

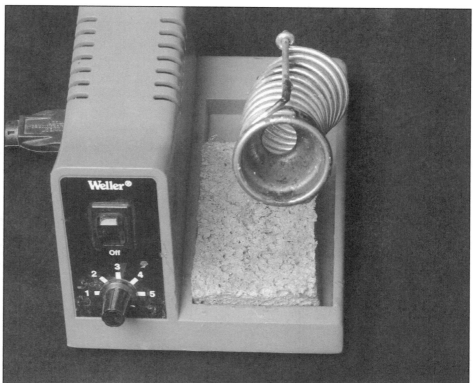

3. Wire strippers.

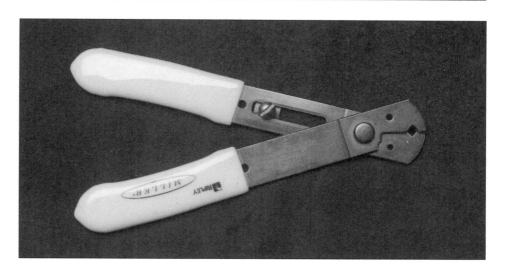

4. Soldering aids (needle-nose pliers, clamps, a vise, etc.).

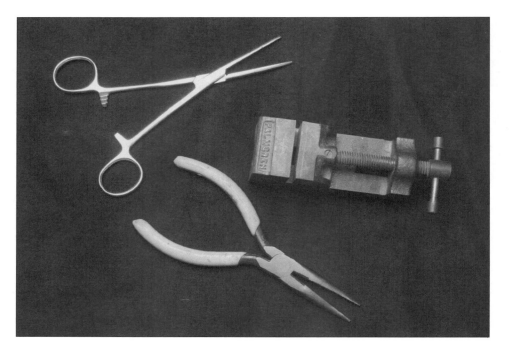

5. High quality solder.

6. Heat shrink tubing (insulating connections) and a butane lighter for heating it.

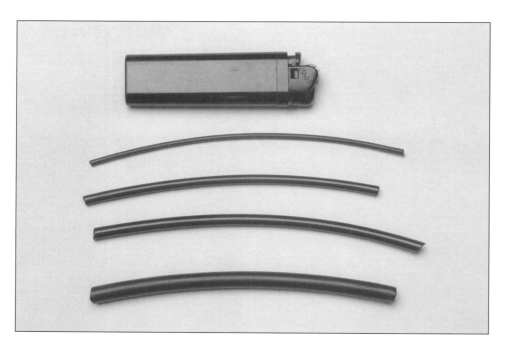

Proper Preparation

One of the primary rules of soldering is cleanliness. Dirt, corrosion, oils or other types of contaminants interfere with the bonding process.

Preparation for Soldering:

1. Make sure that the surfaces to be joined are as clean as possible. You can use a fine sandpaper to clean them.

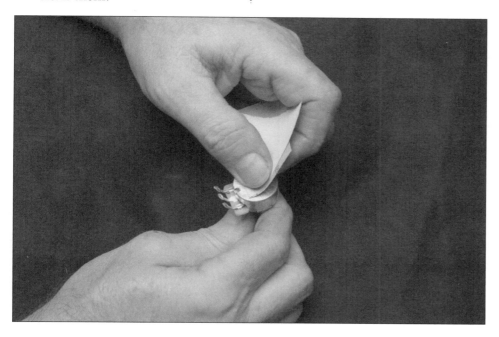

2. Insulation on the wire must be stripped back with wire strippers.

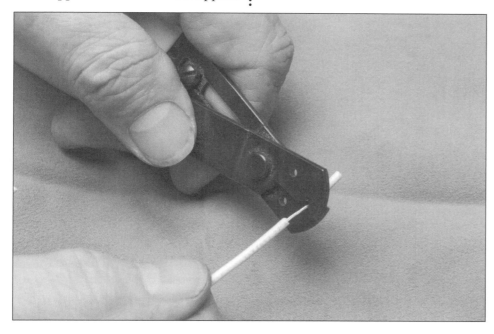

3. The pieces to be soldered must
    be held in close proximity to
    each other.

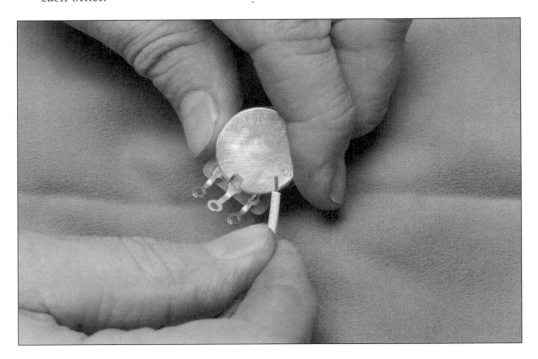

NOTE

*Soldering aids are very useful
for holding and positioning the
parts to be soldered. Be sure
that the aids are not located too
close to the joint area, as they
will dissipate heat and make
soldering more difficult.*

CAUTION

*Soldering irons and molten solder are very hot. To
avoid being burned or damaging the finish on your
guitar, caution should be used in handling this
equipment. Place thin cardboard shields over areas
of the guitar that could be exposed to damage.*

An ounce of prevention is worth a pound of cure!

The Soldering Process

Step 1: Before attempting to solder, it is very important to clean the soldering iron tip. Let your iron come to full temperature, then wipe the tip on a damp cellulose sponge.

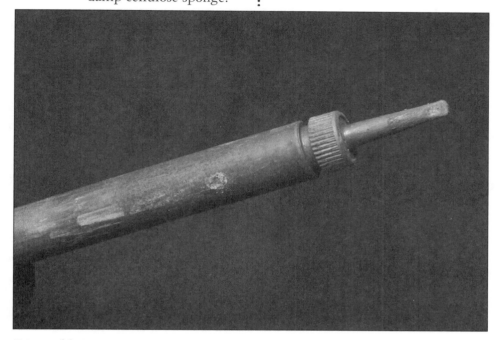

Dirty soldering iron.

Cleaning the soldering iron.

Step 2: To facilitate easier soldering, pre-coat each part with solder. Use the tip of the iron to apply heat directly to the metal being soldered. Touch the solder to a heated part.

When the part is hot enough, the solder will melt and coat it. This should be done to both surfaces prior to joining. This process is known as *tinning*.

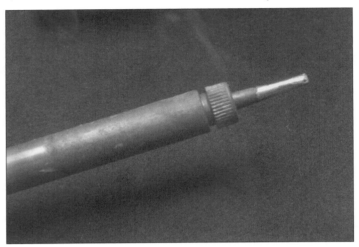

Tin the soldering iron.

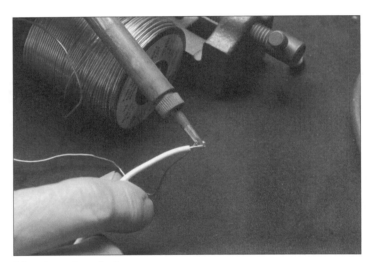

Tin the stripped wire.

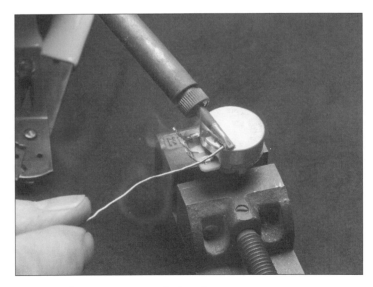

Tin the other part. Notice the handy vise.

Step 3: Place both parts in close proximity to each other and apply heat to both simultaneously.

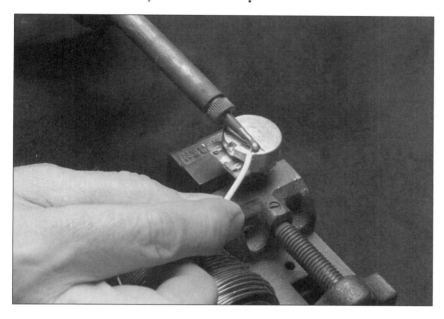

Sometimes it is necessary to apply a little more solder to get a good joint.

Be careful not to move the parts until the solder has cooled. Remember, the closer the proximity the better the joint.

The most common problem with soldering is a *cold joint*. This is caused by not getting the metals to be joined to a high enough temperature. The other common problem is a bad joint due to dirty surfaces.

In addition to repairing connections, your newly acquired soldering skills can be used to install new pickups, *active electronics* (circuitry that requires batteries) or repair patch cords.

Insulation

In some cases, it may be necessary to insulate splices or solder joints that come in close proximity to other components. This is best accomplished with the use of *heat shrink tubing*. Heat shrink tubing is an insulating material that comes in different diameters and colors. Prior to soldering, pick a piece of tubing long enough to cover the affected area. Slip the tubing over the wire. Make sure it is far enough back to avoid premature shrinkage from heat caused by the soldering iron. After the joint has cooled, slide the shrink tubing over the joint and apply a heat source, such as a butane lighter.

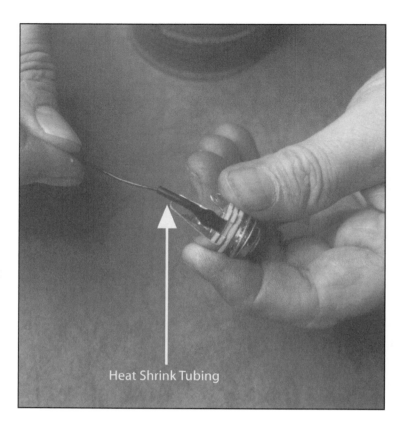

Heat Shrink Tubing

Cleaning and Lubricating Components

Potentiometers ("pots"—the dials you turn to adjust tone and volume) and switches are subject to corrosion. You may have noticed a crackling sound when you turn the knobs or activate switches. This can be very aggravating. In many cases, a simple cleaning and lubricating is all that is necessary. Electronic stores carry contact spray cleaners and lubricants.

The cleaning and lubricating process is as follows:

Step 1: Insert the extension tube into the spray nozzle.

Step 2: Insert the extension tube into the opening in the pot casing and spray. Rotate the knob several times in quick succession.

Step 3: Repeat this procedure with the lubricant.

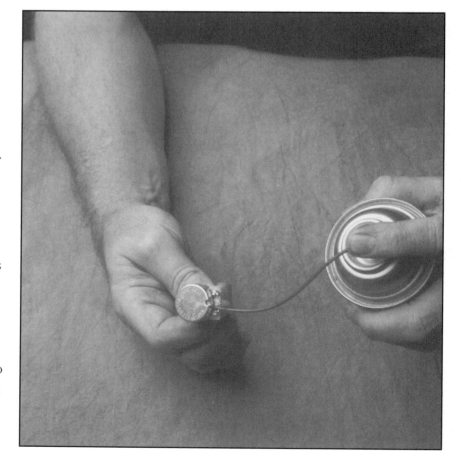

YOUR SETUP

By now, you may have experimented and decided on exactly the right setup for each of your instruments. Here is a chart for you to fill in and keep track of this information. Use a pencil, as you may change your mind from time to time.

Have fun!

Guitar	String	Action	Nut Action	Truss Rod

SETTING UP AND ADJUSTING YOUR FLOYD ROSE SYSTEM

INTRODUCTION

Many players, inspired by the "whammy masters," rushed out and purchased guitars equipped with Floyd Rose tremolo systems of one kind or another. Unfortunately, they receive little or no information on the proper use and maintenance of the product.

Floyd Rose tremolos can create some miraculous effects in the hands of the right player. They can also be a nightmare. The first time you break a string and find that your whole guitar has gone out of tune in the middle of a performance can be more than a little disconcerting. This is why it is important to understand and maintain your system for maximum performance and reliability. The simplest operation, such as restringing, can turn into a disaster resulting in a trip to the guitar repair shop. Hardly a week goes by in my shop without a new guitar owner coming in with a minor disaster. Adjusting the action and intonation are tasks that players should be able to do for themselves.

After 30 plus years of working on instruments, I have written this section to enlighten players and technicians alike about working on guitars equipped with Floyd Rose tremolos.

Even if you prefer to have a tech work on your guitar, it doesn't hurt to know what's involved.

Hopefully you will agree this section is presented in a clear, step-by-step manner and arranged in the proper sequence to obtain optimal results. We have included many photos, drawings and charts to further enhance your understanding. Finally, we have included a diagnostic section to help pinpoint specific problems and their solutions.

My sincerest wish is make your playing more enjoyable and a lot less complicated.

HISTORY OF THE MODERN TREMOLO

The early tremolos were designed in the late forties and early fifties by people like Paul Bigsby and Leo Fender. The name "tremolo" was a misnomer for "vibrato." Vibrato is a change in pitch. Tremolo is a change in volume. However, through constant misuse, the name tremolo became the accepted name.

Early tremolos were okay for subtle effects but caused tuning problems when overused.

Beginnings of the Floyd Rose Tremolo

Floyd Rose, a young guitarist machinist, could see that players like Eddie Van Halen, Steve Vai, Brad Gillis and many others were experiencing difficulty keeping their guitars in tune when using their conventional tremolo systems to the extreme. As a result, he designed the original version of the Floyd Rose Tremolo in the 1970's.

Floyd Rose decided that he could improve the original Fender design. He found several problems in the original design. The strings moved across the nut and bridge saddles when the tremolo was activated. When the tremolo returned to the neutral position the strings didn't. The method for pivoting the bridge assembly was crude and involved too much friction. These factors made it nearly impossible to keep the guitar in tune. He decided to lock the strings at the nut and the bridge. Then he used a knife edge pivot to eliminate friction.

The early models didn't have fine tuners. This made trying to get the guitar in tune very difficult. The player had to guess how much to detune the guitar to compensate for the sharping or flattening effect of the nut clamps when they were tightened. To deal with this problem a new model was designed that had fine tuners. It could be tuned after the strings were locked.

The next significant modification was to lower the position of the fine tuners so that a player's hand wouldn't put the guitar out of tune by resting against the bridge assembly.

With these improvements, the Floyd Rose tremolo proved to hold tune better than any other tremolo sytem.

Due to the effectiveness of the Floyd Rose system, many manufacturers licensed the design and came out with their own versions. They include Fender, Gotoh, Ibanez, Schaller, Takeuchi, Yamaha and many others.

FEATURES

The Floyd Rose tremolo features:

1. A locking nut.

2. Locking saddles.

3. Knife edge pivots (see #7 in the
    illustration on page 61).

4. Fine tuners

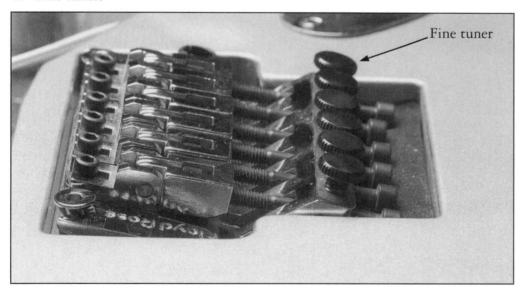

UNDERSTANDING THE BASIC PRINCIPLES OF OPERATION

Before you can use the Floyd Rose tremolo properly, you must understand how the system works. The principals that make the Floyd Rose tremolo stay in tune also make setting up, stringing and playing different than conventional tremolos.

The Floyd Rose tremolo works on the same principle as a balance beam scale. The tension of the strings (on one side of the scale) is offset by the springs (on the other side of the scale). If you change string tension, then you must adjust the springs to match. This is what makes the Floyd Rose tremolo extremely sensitive.

NOTE

Tension can be affected by increasing or decreasing string gauge, or by tuning above or below normal pitch.

On the facing page is an illustration of the parts of a Floyd Rose system. Each part is labeled with a number. The names of the parts, and their corresponding numbers, are listed below.

#	Parts Description
1	Fine tuner
2	String lock bolts
3	Base plate mounting bolt
4	Saddle lock bolt
5	Clamp blocks
6	Saddle assembly
7	Knife edge pivot
8	Pivot stud (wood screw base)
9	Pivot stud (machine bolt)
10	Pivot stud body insert
11	Fine tuner spring assembly
12	Sustain block
13	Springs
14	Claw mounting screws
15	Claw
16	String retainer assembly
17	Nut mounting bolts
18	Lock washers
19	Nut shim
20	Nut
21	Nut caps
22	Nut lock bolts
23	Tremolo arm bushing
24	Base plate
25	Tremolo arm

Nut-Related Parts

Floyd Rose System Parts

See page 60 for part names.

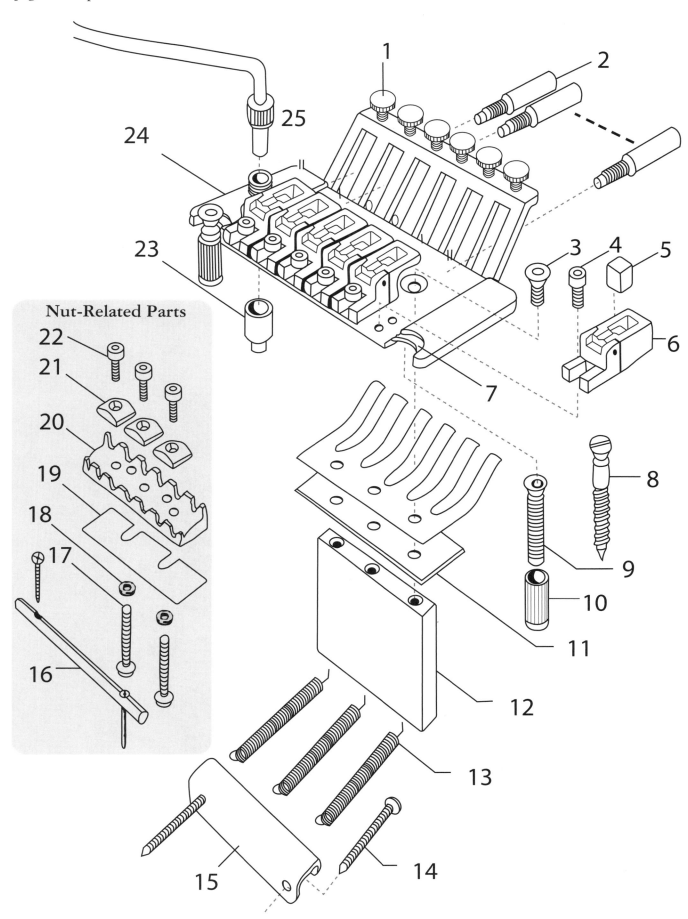

Nut-Related Parts

STRINGING YOUR FLOYD ROSE TREMOLO

The first step to setting up and adjusting your Floyd Rose tremolo is to learn how to properly install the strings.

Steps for removal:

Step 1: Insert shim under back of tremolo. Push the tremolo arm in to insert a spacer just thick enough to keep the tremolo in level position between the face of the guitar and the bottom of the tremolo. Use a material that won't damage the guitar's finish (for example, bottle cork). This will stabilize the tremolo at its neutral position, allowing easy access to the string lock bolts. It will also make tuning the new strings much easier.

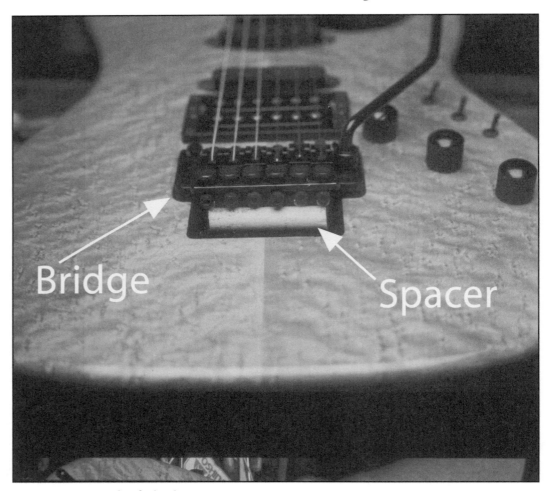

Insert a spacer under the bridge.

Step 2: Loosen nut locks and remove caps.

Step 3: De-tune old strings.

Step 4: Loosen string locks.

Step 5: Remove old strings

Installing New Strings
There are two accepted methods for
stringing Floyd Rose tremolos:

Method 1: Insert the string through
the tuning machine
without removing the
ball end.

Method 2: Cut off the ball end just
above the over-winding
and to insert the string
into the saddle.

Method 1
Step 1: Insert the plain end of the
string through the tuning
machine capstan hole and
pull it through, bringing the
ball end near the capstan.

Step 2: Run the string under the
string retainer and over the
nut.

Step 3: Pull up any slack until
the ball end seats firmly
against the tuning
machine capstan.

Step 4: Stretch the string past the saddle. Then with side cutters cut the string even with the back of the saddle.

Step 5: Insert the string between the loosened clamp lock and the saddle.

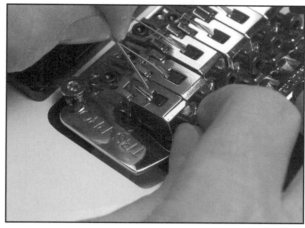

Step 6: Tighten the clamp lock screw.

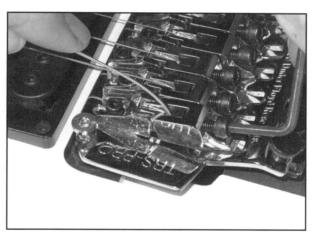

Step 7: Tune to pitch.

Method 2

Step 1: Cut off the ball end just above the over-winding.

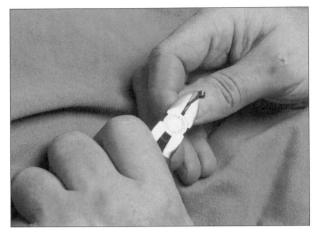

Step 2: Insert the string between the clamp lock and the saddle.

Step 3: Run the string down the neck, over the nut and under the string retainer.

Step 4: Insert the string through the tuning machine capstan.

Step 5: Leave about 3–4 inches of slack.

Step 6: Lock the string as shown below. For "six-in-line" headstocks, lock the strings as for the left side.

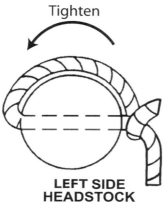

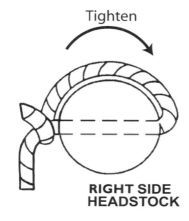

Step 7: Tune to pitch.

After you have completed the restringing, loosen the fine tuners to nearly the full out position.

To stretch each string, pull the string away from the fingerboard about an inch while moving up and down the string. Do this about three or four times to each string. Retune to pitch.

Replace the nut clamps, noting the proper direction (see drawing on right). Remove the shim.

Nut Clamps Orientation

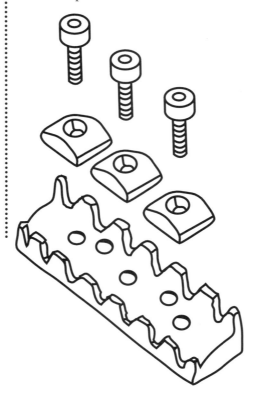

To eliminate problems, there are a couple of basic rules to keep in mind.

1. Make sure that the old broken string ends are removed before installing new ones.

2. Do not over-tighten clamp lock bolts. Over tightening can damage the clamp blocks or the saddle housing.

Also, be aware that:

1. Clamp blocks that have been over-tightened will split and wedge. This will make string insertion very difficult if not impossible.

2. Saddles are susceptible to fracture from over-tightening, and could require costly replacement.

3. Nut lock caps that are over-tightened cause dents in the nut. This can interfere with proper locking.

ADJUSTING YOUR TRUSS ROD

Adjusting the truss rod on a guitar with a Floyd Rose system is the same as the procedure described on pages 13–17.

CAUTION

Use great care when making truss rod adjustments. Normally no more than a half turn is required.

ANGLE OF THE BASE PLATE

After the truss rod has been properly adjusted, it is necessary to adjust the angle of the base plate in relation to the front of the guitar. This is very important because a change in angle can cause a change in action. Normally, the bridge assembly is set parallel to the face of the guitar.

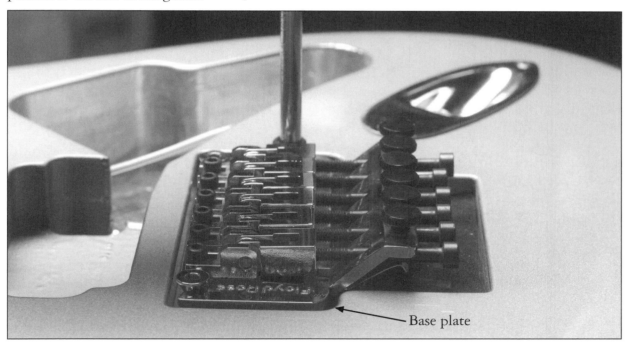

Base plate

This is ideal for two reasons:

1. When making string-length adjustments for intonation, the action will stay the same.

2. You can use this as a visual reference that your guitar is in tune.

Setting the Base Plate Angle

If your base plate isn't parallel to the front of the guitar, it will be necessary to make some adjustments to the spring's tension in the back of your guitar. If the tremolo is tilted away from the front of your guitar, the springs must be tightened. Conversely, if the tremolo is tilted toward the front of your guitar, the springs must be loosened.

Steps for setting base plate angle:

Step 1: Remove the spring cavity cover, exposing the springs. Note the two adjusting screws on the claw.

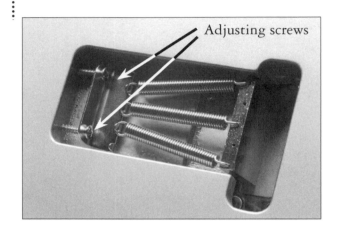

Step 2: To increase spring tension, turn the screws in a clockwise direction. To decrease spring tension, turn the screws in a counterclockwise direction. Note that the claw should be parallel to the edge of the cavity in which it sits.

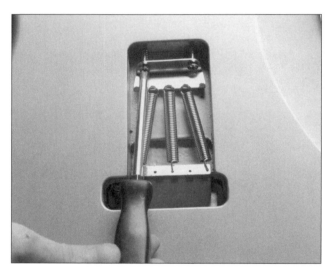

In some cases it may be necessary to add or remove a spring to achieve the proper balance.

Increases in string gauge require more spring tension, while decreases in string gauge require less spring tension. Make sure that all the springs are matched to each other. Variances in length or tension will interfere with proper operation of the tremolo.

CAUTION

Make adjustments in small increments.

It is very important to retune after each adjustment to properly evaluate the base plate position.

Once the base plate is level and the guitar is tuned to the proper pitch, we can proceed with the action adjustment procedures.

SETTING ACTION AT THE BRIDGE

Adjusting the pivot stud on each side of the bridge sets overall action height. Clockwise adjustment lowers the bridge and counter-clockwise raises the bridge.

Some Ibanez pivot posts have internal locking screws that must be released before making adjustments, or you may damage the guitar.

The Procedure

Step 1: With a 6" (or 15 cm) rule, graduated in 64ths, measure the distance from the bottom of the string to the top of the 12th fret. This is done on the 1st and 6th strings. Refer to the chart on page 20 for the actual specifications.

Step 2: Adjust the pivot post on the 1st string to specification.

Step 3: Adjust the pivot post on the 6th string to specification.

Step 4: Measure the action of the in-between strings (2nd, 3rd, 4th and 5th strings).

Step 5: If the action specifications in the chart don't match the measurements that you have taken, it will be necessary to shim the saddles. See page 72 for information about shimming the saddles.

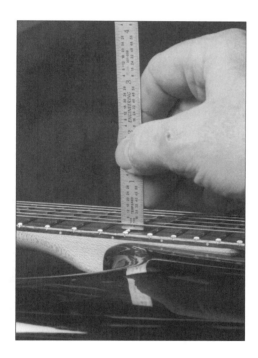

Shimming the Saddles

To gauge the size of the shims that you need, double the difference between the specification and the actual measurement. For example, if you measured the height of the 3rd string (G) saddle and it was too low by _ ", then it would be necessary to put in a shim that is $1/32$" to achieve the right height.

Most Floyd Rose tremolos come with a fixed *radius** (11" or 27.94 cm). This radius is set by having saddles of different height, or by putting steps in the base plate. In some cases, this may not conform to the curvature of the guitar's fingerboard. The easiest way to re-radius the bridge is to place thin metal shims under the saddles.

NOTE

It is a good idea to completely loosen the string before inserting the shims. Also take note of the position of the saddle in regard to string length, so that you may put it back in the same place as it was. Before moving on to the next saddle, retune the string that was attached to the saddle you just shimmed.

In cases where the fingerboard radius is less than the bridge's radius, the middle saddles must be shimmed. When the fingerboard radius is greater than the bridge's, the outside saddles must be shimmed. These shims can be purchased from luthier suppliers, guitar repairmen or you can make your own from shim stock. Shim stock is available from industrial suppliers.

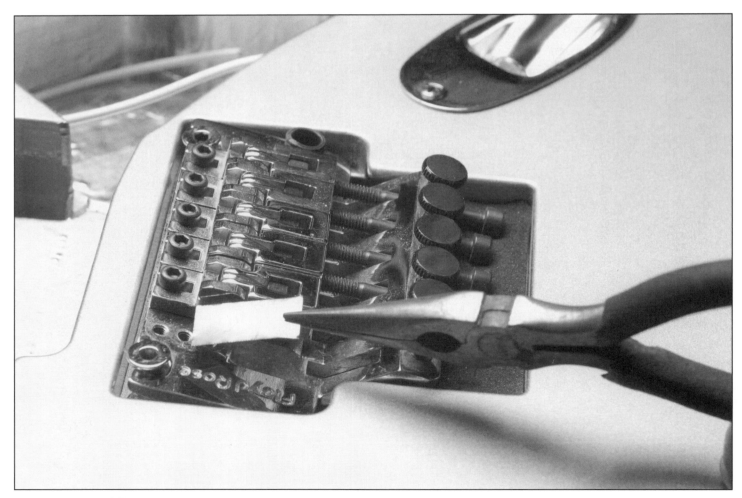

Shimming a saddle.

* "Radius" refers to a convex curvature.

ABOUT THE FLOYD ROSE NUT

Floyd Rose nuts also have a fixed radius. Some manufacturers offer more than one radius, as well as different widths and string spacing. There are some special nuts that are made to accommodate *bullet truss rod* nut adjustments. Introduced in 1966, the bullet truss rod allows Fender-style necks to be adjusted at the headstock—without removing the neck.

Floyd Rose nuts are also available left-handed. On some models, the nut has bolts that go all the way through the neck. On others, the nut is attached from the top by wood screws. There is a photo of a Floyd Rose nut assembly on page 58.

2. If your action is lower than spec, you will have to shim the nut. Sometimes it may be necessary to use different height shims on the bass and treble ends. If your action is too high, you may have to remove some shims. Sometimes there are no shims to remove. In this case it will be necessary to remove some wood from under the nut (an experienced technician should do this).

3. After inserting or removing the appropriate shims, be sure to tighten the bolts or screws.

Setting Nut Height

After setting the action at the bridge, the next step is to set the action at the nut. The Floyd Rose nut action is set by putting shims between the nut and the mating surface on the neck.

In some cases, the curvature of the nut doesn't conform to that of the fingerboard. If the radius of the nut is smaller than that of the fingerboard, it usually doesn't present a problem. If the curvature is greater than that of the fingerboard, the strings in the middle may be too low when the outside strings are normal. This problem can be dealt with in two ways:
1. Get a nut that has the correct radius.
2. Shim the nut higher than normal

The first method is the best approach when possible. The second approach makes playing in the 1st position more difficult and aversely affects the intonation.

Steps for setting the nut height:

1. Using a feeler gauge, measure the space between the first fret and the bottom of the string. The normal nut action should be .018" or (.04572 cm). If the .018" blade is too tight or too loose, use a thinner or thicker blade until you find the size that fits. The difference between the two blades will determine the shim size. This should be done on the 1st and 6th strings.

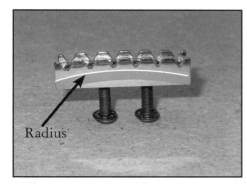

Radius

This is just one possible nut radius.

Setting the String Retainer

After the nut has been properly adjusted, the string retainer should also be reset. The string retainer keeps the strings seated in the nut so that the strings are not sharpened when the nut clamps are locked. The string retainer has a screw at either end. These screws set the height of the string retainer. When the string retainer bar is set properly, the high and low "E" strings should just conform to the top of the nut surface.

SETTING INTONATION (STRING LENGTH)

The final step in adjusting your Floyd Rose tremolo is to set the intonation. Because of differences in the flexibility of individual strings, it is necessary to set the vibrating length of each string. This will insure that your guitar will play in tune from note to note and key to key throughout its playing range. Intonation adjustments should be made using an electronic tuner. But if you have a good ear, you may be able to get by.

Steps for setting the intonation:

Step 1: Loosen the nut clamps.

Step 2: Plug your guitar into the electronic tuner and turn it on.

Step 3: Tune all the open strings to the tuner.

Step 4: Start with the 6th (low E) string. Play the harmonic at the 12th fret and then play the fretted octave at the 12th fret. Note if the fretted note is sharp or flat. If the note is flat the string is too long and must be shortened. Conversely, if the note is sharp the string must be lengthened.

Step 5: To make the appropriate adjustments without specialized tools, you must loosen the string and unlock the saddle mounting screw.

Step 6: Slide the saddle in the correct direction to compensate for the tuning error: toward the nut to shorten the string, away from the nut to lengthen it. After a bit of practice you will be able to judge approximately how much to move the saddles in relation to the amount of error.

Step 7: Relock the saddle screw and retune the string. Check the open 12th fret harmonic against the fretted octave. If they are the same, proceed to the next string. If not, repeat the procedure until they are.

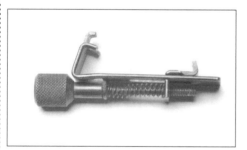

There is a company that makes a tool that clips on to the back of the bridge and the string lock screw, allowing you to make saddle adjustments without detuning. This is very handy and can save a lot of time.

TREMOLO ARM ASSEMBLY

The older Floyd Rose tremolo had an arm that threaded into a bushing mounted on the base plate. To allow movement of the arm, there was a nylon washer on each side of the base plate. This system had a bad habit of working itself loose. A wrench was needed to remove the arm. Later models featured a new arm design that could be tensioned from the top to control arm movement. This also made it possible to remove the arm with your fingers.

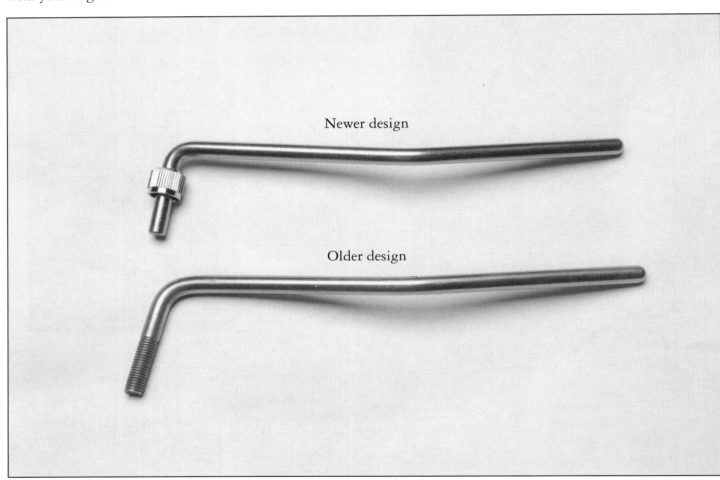

Newer design

Older design

ADDENDUM A

TOOLS REQUIRED FOR ADJUSTING YOUR FLOYD ROSE TREMOLO

A few basic tools are required to adjust the Floyd Rose tremolo.

You will require the following:

1. One Phillips #2 screwdriver (spring claw screws)

2. One straight blade screwdriver (pivot post)

3. One 3 mm Allen wrench (nut and saddle string locks)

4. One 2.5 mm Allen wrench (nut mounting bolts)

5. One 2 mm Allen wrench (saddle lock bolts)

6. One 1.5 mm Allen wrench (pivot stud lock screws for Ibanez models)

7. 6" or 15 cm rule graduated in 64ths" or mm (action measurements)

8. One automotive feeler gauge set (nut and truss rod measurements)

9. Two 11 mm open end wrenches (tensioning original style arm)

10. One pair of shears (cutting shim material)

11. One electronic tuner with cord (setting intonation)

Feeler gauges.

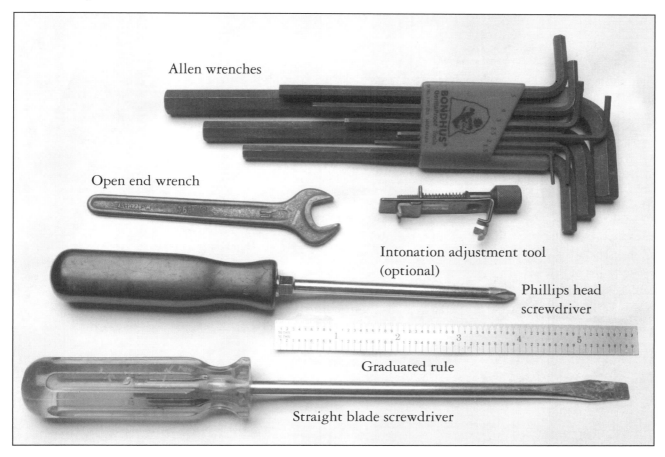

Allen wrenches

Open end wrench

Intonation adjustment tool (optional)

Phillips head screwdriver

Graduated rule

Straight blade screwdriver

ADDENDUM B

TROUBLESHOOTING THE FLOYD ROSE TREMOLO

Problem: String buzzing.

Probable causes:

1. Worn out strings

2. Back bowed neck

3. Pickups set too high

4. Wear in the nut or saddle

5. Fret buzz

6. Strings not clamped properly

7. Defective casting on the nut or saddle

Solutions:

1. Examine the strings for wear or corrosion. Replace if necessary. Re-check for buzz.

2. Check truss rod adjustment. Reset if necessary.

3. Fret the string at the last fret. Visually inspect the space between the pickup and the string. Lower if necessary.

4. Inspect the area where the string contacts the nut and saddle. If wear marks or corrosion are present replace the part.

5. Examine the frets for wear. Observe if the buzzing only occurs in a specific area. Dress and re-round or replace the frets.

6. The string should be clamped in the middle of the nut and saddle slots. To determine if you have a nut or saddle buzz fret the string at the first fret. If the buzz stops, the buzz is at the nut.

7. Replace the defective part.

Problem: Excessive string breakage.

Solution:

1. Replace worn out strings.

2. Avoid over-tightening the string clamp at the nut.

3. Excessive string breakage can be caused by corrosion at the string contact point of the nut or saddle. Replace worn or corroded parts.

Problem: Tremolo can't be adjusted to sit parallel to the face of the guitar with claw adjustment all the way in.

Solution:

1. The string gauge may be excessive for the amount of springs counteracting the force. Add more springs as needed.

2. The springs may have been over-extended causing them to be damaged. If this is the case, they should be replaced.

Remember: The springs should match each other.

Problem: The guitar won't stay in tune.

Solution:

1. The strings need to be stretched.

2. Check to see if nut clamps are properly locked.

3. Check for grooves in the nut and nut clamps. Replace if necessary.

4. Check nut-mounting bolts for tightness.

5. Check intonation adjustments.

6. Check for loose neck screws.

7. Check springs for mismatch or contact with the body or back plate.

8. Check pivot studs, and knife-edges for excess wear.

9. Check for loose pivot studs or misalignment.

10. Check for magnetic pull from the pickups. Lower pickups.

Problem: Fine tuners won't adjust.

Solution:

(1) Saddle pivot points corroded. Lubricate.

Problem: Height adjustment screws are bottomed out, but the action is still too high.

Solution:

1. This problem is caused by insufficient neck angle. It can be remedied by removing the neck and placing a shim inbetween the neck pocket and the heel of the neck.

2. One other solution is to cut a recess in the front of the guitar provided that it doesn't already have one.

Problem: When I use my tremolo, the springs make noise.

Solution:

1. Coat the springs with silicon RTV.

2. Lubricate the spring attachment points.

Helpful Hint
Some players would rather have tuning stability than be able to pull up on their tremolo. This can accomplished by blocking the tremolo so that the arm works only in the down mode.

Steps:

1. Make a block of wood just thick enough to fit between the sustain block and the edge of the spring cavity when the tremolo is in the rest position. Glue a thin layer of felt or hard rubber on the side of the block facing the sustain block. This will eliminate body noise when the tremolo returns to the neutral position.

2. Glue the block of wood in place between the sustain block and the edge of the spring cavity.

3. Tighten the claw adjustment screws, until you can bend notes without the tremolo pulling away from the body.

This modification will keep the guitar in tune even if a string should break. It is also useful for players who bend notes against pedal tones.

Congratulations! You have reached the end of *Teach Yourself Guitar Maintenance and Repair*. You've learned a lot, but there's lots more to know. Let an expert handle the really tricky procedures and be very careful with your guitar. Enjoy!